Betty Lou's Bad Mood Blues

Jocelyn Stevenson
Illustrations by Arkadia

in association with Channel Four Television

FANTAIL BOOKS
Published by the Penguin Group
Penguin Books Ltd, 27 Wrights Lane, London W8 5TZ, England
Penguin Books USA Inc., 375 Hudson Street, New York, New York 10014, USA
Penguin Books Australia Ltd, Ringwood, Victoria, Australia
Penguin Books Canada Ltd, 10 Alcorn Avenue, Toronto, Ontario, Canada M4V 3B2
Penguin Books (NZ) Ltd, 182-190 Wairau Road, Auckland 10, New Zealand

Penguin Books Ltd, Registered Offices: Harmondsworth, Middlesex, England

First published 1992
1 3 5 7 9 10 8 6 4 2

Set in Monotype Times New Roman Schoolbook

Printed and bound in Italy by Imago Publishing

Betty Lou was in the middle of the best dream she had ever had when her mother woke her up. The dream disappeared. Betty looked at her clock. "It's not time to get up!" she grumbled.

Betty Lou's mother opened the curtains. "I'm sorry, Betty Lou, but we have to leave early for school today," said her mother. "I have to collect something from town."

Betty Lou frowned and dragged herself out of bed. "Come and eat your breakfast now," said her mother.

"I want to wash up the dishes while you're getting dressed." Then she left the room. Betty Lou was not happy. She did not like eating breakfast in her pyjamas on school days.

It's no good feeling grumpy and unhappy when you need to eat your breakfast. That kind of feeling can make you forget to stop putting cereal into your bowl until it's too late. Then it can let you pour orange juice on your cereal instead of milk. That's exactly what Betty Lou's feeling did to her. She looked at her cereal, floating in orange juice. The grumpy feeling started to grow.

Betty Lou decided not to have cereal after all. "Toast with honey, that's what I want," she said. She reached for the honey. But she hadn't put the lid on properly the last time she'd used it. The lid stayed in her hand while the jar fell to the floor.

Betty Lou cleaned up the gooey mess. The unhappy feeling grew even bigger. This is going to be a bad day, she thought.

Betty Lou went to get dressed. She accidentally chose the jumper with the very tight neck, but didn't notice until she got stuck. She had to take it off and put a dress on instead. Then she put on her socks. At least they didn't give me any trouble, she thought. And then she saw that all the knobbly bits were on the outside of the socks. Betty pulled them off and started again.

"Hurry up, Betty Lou! It's time to go!" called her mother. Betty Lou pulled on her shoes quickly, without bothering to tie the laces. She grabbed her coat and school-bag and ran out of the door.

As Betty Lou raced towards the car, she tripped over her laces. The last thing you need when you're feeling rushed and grumpy is to fall flat on your face. Betty Lou's mother helped her up. Betty Lou's unhappy feeling grew bigger and bigger.

By the time Betty Lou was strapped up in the back of the car, she was so upset she could hardly speak. Her mother glanced at her through the rear-view mirror. "What a face!" she said. "Is something the matter, Betty Lou?"

"No," growled Betty Lou.

"Well, we're early for school, so you'll have Mrs Ferguson all to yourself," said her mother, trying to cheer her up.

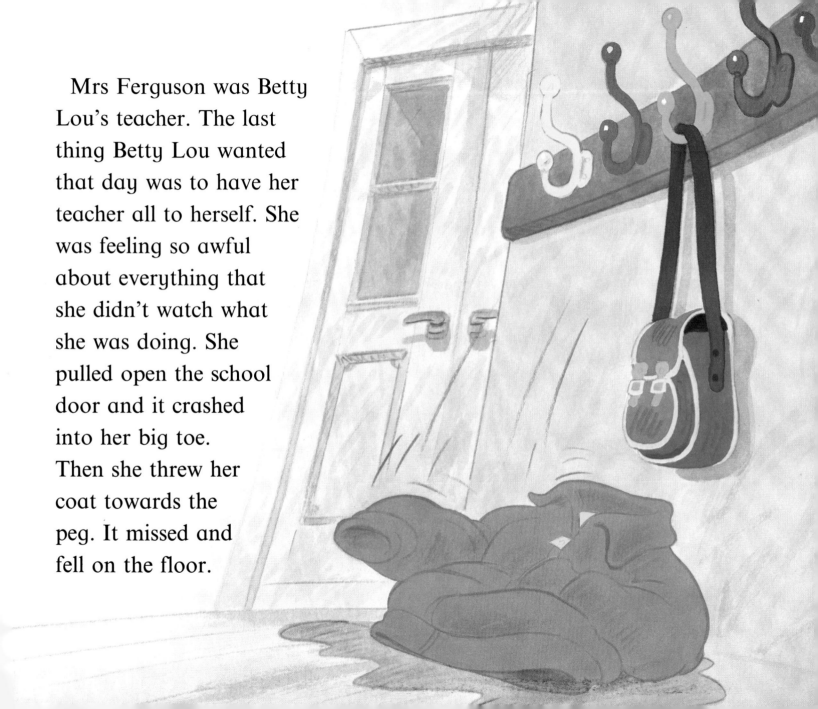

Mrs Ferguson was Betty Lou's teacher. The last thing Betty Lou wanted that day was to have her teacher all to herself. She was feeling so awful about everything that she didn't watch what she was doing. She pulled open the school door and it crashed into her big toe. Then she threw her coat towards the peg. It missed and fell on the floor.

Betty Lou walked into Mrs Ferguson's room. "You look as if you got out of the wrong side of bed this morning," said Mrs Ferguson.

That's just the sort of silly thing grown-ups say, thought Betty Lou.

Betty Lou tried to draw, but she pushed too hard on the red crayon she was using. It broke and spoilt her picture. Then she made a tower using all the building bricks. The problem was, she built it too close to the classroom door. When the other children started coming in, someone knocked it over by mistake. Then she went to find her favourite doll, but somebody else was playing with it.

Betty Lou went into the toilet.

By the time Betty Lou returned to the class, Mrs Ferguson had already begun to read the morning's story. Betty Lou had to sit at the back, too far away to see the pictures. This is the worst day I've ever, ever had, she thought.

When the class went outside to play, Betty Lou stood by the wall.
By now, the bad feeling was so big, it filled her up. It made her want

to scream and cry. But she didn't
want to do any of these
things in front of
her friends and
teacher. So she
just stood
by herself,
feeling
terrible.

It was snacktime. Usually Betty Lou loved having a snack. But on this horrible day she wasn't hungry. The horrid feeling inside her was taking up too much space. There was only enough room left for a glass of milk. Betty Lou carried her glass carefully back to her seat. She was just about to sit down when it happened. Herry accidentally bumped into her. Betty Lou spilled the milk over her feet.

"I'm sorry," she heard Herry say, as he mopped at the milk with a cloth. "It was an accident."

"THAT'S IT!" Betty Lou shouted suddenly. "I AM ANGRY! VERY ANGRY! I'VE BEEN FEELING ANGRY ALL DAY!"

Betty Lou could see everyone staring
at her, but she didn't care. The angry
feeling had to come out. "And do
you know what makes me feel
angriest?" she said. Herry shook
his head. "It's when I'm so angry
that I can't even say I feel angry.
That makes me feel really
angry!"

"But you've just said you feel
angry," said Herry, trying to
be helpful. "Why don't you
say it again?"

"I FEEL ANGRY!" cried
Betty Lou.

"Say it again!" said the rest of the class. Betty Lou took a deep breath and was just about to scream "I feel angry" again, when she realized that the gigantic feeling had gone. Suddenly, a calm, peaceful feeling filled up the place where the angry feeling had been. Betty Lou smiled. "I don't feel angry any more," she said. "Thanks, Herry!"

"Don't mention it!" said Herry.

And the two of them wiped up the mess and played happily together until it was time for the next lesson to begin.